Responsibility

DISNEP'S
THE
LION KING

Adapted by T.J. Dugan
Illustrated by the Disney Storybook Artists

Published by Louis Weber, C.E.O.
Publications International, Ltd.
7373 North Cicero Avenue, Lincolnwood, Illinois 60712

Ground Floor, 59 Gloucester Place, London W1U 8JJ
Customer Service: 1-800-595-8484 or customer_service@pilbooks.com

www.pilbooks.com

p i kids is a registered trademark of Publications International, Ltd.

ISBN-13: 978-1-4127-6244-1
ISBN-10: 1-4127-6244-8

All the animals from the Pride Lands gathered. There were eagles and ostriches, antelope and elephants. They came to get a good look as Rafiki, the wise baboon, lifted the Lion King's cub for all to see. His name was Simba and he would someday be their king. The animals cheered!

But not everyone celebrated Mufasa and Sarabi's cub. Scar, Mufasa's own brother, was very jealous. Scar wanted to be king.

"One day, Simba, the sun will set on my time here and will rise with you as the new king," Mufasa said. He explained that all the animals had an important place in the Circle of Life.

Simba couldn't wait to be king! He even bragged about it to his Uncle Scar.

"Everywhere the sun shines will be my kingdom!" Simba said. "Everywhere, except the shadowy place. My father said I'm not supposed to go there."

Scar saw a chance to trick Simba. "Only brave lions go there," Scar said.

Simba knew he shouldn't go, but he wanted to be brave. He and his friend Nala set out to explore the mysterious shadowy place.

Three mean hyenas were waiting for them!
Simba and Nala were trapped. Just then they
heard a giant roar. Mufasa came to rescue them!

Mufasa was angry at his young cub.

"I just wanted to be brave," Simba said.

"Doing foolish things isn't brave," Mufasa
said. "Being brave means you understand
your responsiblity to do what is right."

Father and son looked up at the
twinkling stars. Mufasa told Simba
that the stars were the great
kings of the past looking down
on them. "Remember, Simba,"
Mufasa said, "those kings
will always be there to
guide you. So will I."

Meanwhile, Scar was angry that Simba had escaped. He ordered the hyenas to start a stampede of wildebeests. Simba was in danger again! When Mufasa came to Simba's rescue, he slipped on the rocks and fell. He was gone forever.

It was an accident, but Scar blamed Simba. "Run away and never come back!" shouted Scar.

Simba ran and ran. He didn't stop until he was deep in the jungle where two friendly animals named Timon and Pumbaa found him and tried to cheer him up. "Our motto is *hakuna matata*," Timon said. "No worries," Pumbaa explained.

It didn't take long for Simba to stop thinking of home. "*Hakuna matata*," he said with a shrug.

The friends spent their days playing and napping in the sun.

One day, a lioness chased Pumbaa. Simba jumped to his rescue. The lioness was Nala, Simba's old friend! After apologizing to Pumbaa, Nala explained how terrible things were in the Pride Lands.

"There's no water
or food," she said. "We need
you! Please come home."

"I can't," Simba said sadly.

"You're our king," she said.

Simba was confused. He had
forgotten his responsibility to
lead and protect the other animals.

But the wise baboon Rafiki hadn't forgotten. He helped Simba to see that he had grown into a brave lion, just like his father.

Simba remembered what his father had told him. He searched the stars for help. Mufasa's face glowed in the moonlight. "Remember who you are," he said.

"I am king," Simba said. He knew that in the Circle of Life, he had an important place and an important responsibility.

Simba and his friends went to the Pride Lands and defeated Scar. The eagles and ostriches, antelope and elephants, and all the other animals cheered. Their king was home!

Responsibility

Being responsible means taking care of what is important. The Lion King had a responsibility to the other animals of the Pride Lands. They counted on him, and they trusted him.

When Simba lived with Timon and Pumbaa, he ignored his responsibility to the Pride Lands. But with help, Simba was able to return and accept his responsibility. He overcame his fears and did the right thing.